CONTAGION

CONTAGION

by Katherine MacLEAN

It was like an Earth forest in the fall, but it was not fall. The forest leaves were green and copper and purple and fiery red, and a wind sent patches of bright greenish sunlight dancing among the leaf shadows.

The hunt party of the *Explorer* filed along the narrow trail, guns ready, walking carefully, listening to the distant, half familiar cries of strange birds.

A faint crackle of static in their earphones indicated that a gun had been fired.

"Got anything?" asked June Walton. The helmet intercom carried her voice to the ears of the others without breaking the stillness of the forest.

"Took a shot at something," explained George Barton's cheerful voice in her earphones. She rounded a bend of the trail and came upon Barton standing peering up into the trees, his gun still raised. "It looked like a duck."

"This isn't Central Park," said Hal Barton, his brother, coming into sight. His green spacesuit struck an incongruous note against the bronze and red forest. "They won't all look like ducks," he said soberly.

"Maybe some will look like dragons. Don't get eaten by a dragon, June," came Max's voice quietly into her earphones. "Not while I still love you." He came out of the trees carrying the blood sample kit, and touched her glove with his, the grin on his ugly beloved face barely visible in the mingled light and shade. A patch of sunlight struck a greenish glint from his fishbowl helmet.

*

They walked on. A quarter of a mile back, the space ship *Explorer* towered over the forest like a tapering skyscraper, and the people of the ship looked out of the viewplates at fresh winds and sunlight and clouds, and they longed to be outside.

But the likeness to Earth was danger, and the cool wind might be death, for if the animals were like Earth animals, their diseases might be like Earth diseases, alike enough to be contagious, different enough to be impossible to treat. There was warning enough in the past. Colonies had vanished, and traveled spaceways drifted with the corpses of ships which had touched on some plague planet.

The people of the ship waited while their doctors, in airtight spacesuits, hunted animals to test them for contagion.

The four medicos, for June Walton was also a doctor, filed through the alien homelike forest, walking softly, watching for motion among the copper and purple shadows.

They saw it suddenly, a lighter moving copper patch among the darker browns. Reflex action swung June's gun into line, and behind her someone's gun went off with a faint crackle of static, and made a hole in the leaves beside the specimen. Then for a while no one moved.

This one looked like a man, a magnificently muscled, leanly graceful, humanlike animal. Even in its callused bare feet, it was a head taller than any of them. Red-haired, hawk-faced and darkly tanned, it stood breathing heavily, looking at them without expression. At its side hung a sheath knife, and a crossbow was slung across one wide shoulder.

They lowered their guns.

"It needs a shave," Max said reasonably in their earphones, and he reached up to his helmet and flipped the switch that let his voice be heard. "Something we could do for you, Mac?"

The friendly drawl was the first voice that had broken the forest sounds. June smiled suddenly. He was right. The strict logic of evolution did not demand beards; therefore a non-human would not be wearing a three day growth of red stubble.

Still panting, the tall figure licked dry lips and spoke. "Welcome to Minos. The Mayor sends greetings from Alexandria."

"English?" gasped June.

"We were afraid you would take off again before I could bring word to you.... It's three hundred miles.... We saw your scout plane pass twice, but we couldn't attract its attention."

*

June looked in stunned silence at the stranger leaning against the tree. Thirty-six light years—thirty-six times six trillion miles of monotonous space travel—to be told that the planet was already settled! "We didn't know there was a colony here," she said. "It is not on the map."

"We were afraid of that," the tall bronze man answered soberly. "We have been here three generations and yet no traders have come."

Max shifted the kit strap on his shoulder and offered a hand. "My name is Max Stark, M.D. This is June Walton, M.D., Hal Barton, M.D., and George Barton, Hal's brother, also M.D."

"Patrick Mead is the name," smiled the man, shaking hands casually. "Just a hunter and bridge carpenter myself. Never met any medicos before."

The grip was effortless but even through her airproofed glove June could feel that the fingers that touched hers were as hard as padded steel.

"What—what is the population of Minos?" she asked.

He looked down at her curiously for a moment before answering. "Only one hundred and fifty." He smiled. "Don't worry, this isn't a city planet yet. There's room for a few more people." He shook hands with the Bartons quickly. "That is—you are people, aren't you?" he asked startlingly.

"Why not?" said Max with a poise that June admired.

"Well, you are all so—so—" Patrick Mead's eyes roamed across the faces of the group. "So varied."

They could find no meaning in that, and stood puzzled.

"I mean," Patrick Mead said into the silence, "all these—interesting different hair colors and face shapes and so forth—" He made a vague wave with one hand as if he had run out of words or was anxious not to insult them.

"Joke?" Max asked, bewildered.

June laid a hand on his arm. "No harm meant," she said to him over the intercom. "We're just as much of a shock to him as he is to us."

She addressed a question to the tall colonist on outside sound. "What should a person look like, Mr. Mead?"

He indicated her with a smile. "Like you."

June stepped closer and stood looking up at him, considering her own description. She was tall and tanned, like him; had a few freckles, like him; and wavy red hair, like his. She ignored the brightly humorous blue eyes.

"In other words," she said, "everyone on the planet looks like you and me?"

Patrick Mead took another look at their four faces and began to grin. "Like me, I guess. But I hadn't thought of it before. I did not think that people could have different colored hair or that noses could fit so many ways onto faces. I was judging by my own appearance, but I suppose any fool can walk on his hands and say the world is upside down!" He laughed and sobered. "But then why wear spacesuits? The air is breathable."

"For safety," June told him. "We can't take any chances on plague."

Pat Mead was wearing nothing but a loin cloth and his weapons, and the wind ruffled his hair. He looked comfortable, and they longed to take off the stuffy spacesuits and feel the wind against their own skins. Minos was like home, like Earth.... But they were strangers.

"Plague," Pat Mead said thoughtfully. "We had one here. It came two years after the colony arrived and killed everyone except the Mead families. They were immune. I guess we look alike because we're all related, and that's why I grew up thinking that it is the only way people can look."

Plague. "What was the disease?" Hal Barton asked.

"Pretty gruesome, according to my father. They called it the melting sickness. The doctors died too soon to find out what it was or what to do about it."

"You should have trained for more doctors, or sent to civilization for some." A trace of impatience was in George Barton's voice.

Pat Mead explained patiently, "Our ship, with the power plant and all the books we needed, went off into the sky to avoid the contagion, and never came back. The crew must have died." Long years of hardship were indicated by that statement, a colony with electric power gone and machinery stilled, with key technicians dead and no way to replace them. June realized then the full meaning of the primitive sheath knife and bow.

"Any recurrence of melting sickness?" asked Hal Barton.

"No."

"Any other diseases?"

"Not a one."

Max was eyeing the bronze red-headed figure with something approaching awe. "Do you think all the Meads look like that?" he said to June on the intercom. "I wouldn't mind being a Mead myself!"

*

Their job had been made easy by the coming of Pat. They went back to the ship laughing, exchanging anecdotes with him. There was nothing now to keep Minos from being the home they wanted, except the melting sickness, and, forewarned against it, they could take precautions.

The polished silver and black column of the *Explorer* seemed to rise higher and higher over the trees as they neared it. Then its symmetry blurred all sense of specific size as they stepped out from among the trees and stood on the edge of the meadow, looking up.

9

"Nice!" said Pat. "Beautiful!" The admiration in his voice was warming.

"It was a yacht," Max said, still looking up, "second hand, an old-time beauty without a sign of wear. Synthetic diamond-studded control board and murals on the walls. It doesn't have the new speed drives, but it brought us thirty-six light years in one and a half subjective years. Plenty good enough."

The tall tanned man looked faintly wistful, and June realized that he had never had access to a full library, never seen a movie, never experienced luxury. He had been born and raised on Minos.

*

"May I go aboard?" Pat asked hopefully.

Max unslung the specimen kit from his shoulder, laid it on the carpet of plants that covered the ground and began to open it.

"Tests first," Hal Barton said. "We have to find out if you people still carry this so-called melting sickness. We'll have to de-microbe you and take specimens before we let you on board. Once on, you'll be no good as a check for what the other Meads might have."

Max was taking out a rack and a stand of preservative bottles and hypodermics.

"Are you going to jab me with those?" Pat asked with interest.

"You're just a specimen animal to me, bud!" Max grinned at Pat Mead, and Pat grinned back. June saw that they were friends already, the tall pantherish colonist, and the wry, black-haired doctor. She felt a stab of guilt because she loved Max and yet could pity him for being smaller and frailer than Pat Mead.

"Lie down," Max told him, "and hold still. We need two spinal fluid samples from the back, a body cavity one in front, and another from the arm."

Pat lay down obediently. Max knelt, and, as he spoke, expertly swabbed and inserted needles with the smooth speed that had made him a fine nerve surgeon on Earth.

10

High above them the scout helioplane came out of an opening in the ship and angled off toward the west, its buzz diminishing. Then, suddenly, it veered and headed back, and Reno Unrich's voice came tinnily from their earphones:

"What's that you've got? Hey, what are you docs doing down there?" He banked again and came to a stop, hovering fifty feet away. June could see his startled face looking through the glass at Pat.

Hal Barton switched to a narrow radio beam, explained rapidly and pointed in the direction of Alexandria. Reno's plane lifted and flew away over the odd-colored forest.

"The plane will drop a note on your town, telling them you got through to us," Hal Barton told Pat, who was sitting up watching Max dextrously put the blood and spinal fluids into the right bottles without exposing them to air.

"We won't be free to contact your people until we know if they still carry melting sickness," Max added. "You might be immune so it doesn't show on you, but still carry enough germs—if that's what caused it—to wipe out a planet."

"If you do carry melting sickness," said Hal Barton, "we won't be able to mingle with your people until we've cleared them of the disease."

"Starting with me?" Pat asked.

"Starting with you," Max told him ruefully, "as soon as you step on board."

"More needles?"

"Yes, and a few little extras thrown in."

"Rough?"

"It isn't easy."

A few minutes later, standing in the stalls for spacesuit decontamination, being buffeted by jets of hot disinfectant, bathed in glares of sterilizing ultraviolet radiation, June remembered that and compared Pat Mead's treatment to theirs.

CONTAGION

In the *Explorer*, stored carefully in sealed tanks and containers, was the ultimate, multi-purpose cureall. It was a solution of enzymes so like the key catalysts of the human cell nucleus that it caused chemical derangement and disintegration in any non-human cell. Nothing could live in contact with it but human cells; any alien intruder to the body would die. Nucleocat Cureall was its trade name.

But the cureall alone was not enough for complete safety. Plagues had been known to slay too rapidly and universally to be checked by human treatment. Doctors are not reliable; they die. Therefore spaceways and interplanetary health law demanded that ship equipment for guarding against disease be totally mechanical in operation, rapid and efficient.

Somewhere near them, in a series of stalls which led around and around like a rabbit maze, Pat was being herded from stall to stall by peremptory mechanical voices, directed to soap and shower, ordered to insert his arm into a slot which took a sample of his blood, given solutions to drink, bathed in germicidal ultraviolet, shaken by sonic blasts, breathing air thick with sprays of germicidal mists, being directed to put his arms into other slots where they were anesthesized and injected with various immunizing solutions.

Finally, he would be put in a room of high temperature and extreme dryness, and instructed to sit for half an hour while more fluids were dripped into his veins through long thin tubes.

All legal spaceships were built for safety. No chance was taken of allowing a suspected carrier to bring an infection on board with him.

*

June stepped from the last shower stall into the locker room, zipped off her spacesuit with a sigh of relief, and contemplated herself in a wall mirror. Red hair, dark blue eyes, tall....

"I've got a good figure," she said thoughtfully.

Max turned at the door. "Why this sudden interest in your looks?" he asked suspiciously. "Do we stand here and admire you, or do we finally get something to eat?"

"Wait a minute." She went to a wall phone and dialed it carefully, using a combination from the ship's directory. "How're you doing, Pat?"

The phone picked up a hissing of water or spray. There was a startled chuckle. "Voices, too! Hello, June. How do you tell a machine to go jump in the lake?"

"Are you hungry?"

"No food since yesterday."

"We'll have a banquet ready for you when you get out," she told Pat and hung up, smiling. Pat Mead's voice had a vitality and enjoyment which made shipboard talk sound like sad artificial gaiety in contrast.

They looked into the nearby small laboratory where twelve squealing hamsters were protestingly submitting to a small injection each of Pat's blood. In most of them the injection was followed by one of antihistaminics and adaptives. Otherwise the hamster defense system would treat all non-hamster cells as enemies, even the harmless human blood cells, and fight back against them violently.

One hamster, the twelfth, was given an extra large dose of adaptive, so that if there were a disease, he would not fight it or the human cells, and thus succumb more rapidly.

"How ya doing, George?" Max asked.

"Routine," George Barton grunted absently.

On the way up the long spiral ramps to the dining hall, they passed a viewplate. It showed a long scene of mountains in the distance on the horizon, and between them, rising step by step as they grew farther away, the low rolling hills, bronze and red with patches of clear green where there were fields.

Someone was looking out, standing very still, as if she had been there a long time—Bess St. Clair, a Canadian woman. "It looks like Winnipeg," she told them as they paused. "When are you doctors going to let us out of this blithering barberpole? Look," she pointed. "See that patch of field on the south hillside, with the brook winding through it? I've staked that hillside for our house. When do we get out?"

*

Reno Ulrich's tiny scout plane buzzed slowly in from the distance and began circling lazily.

"Sooner than you think," Max told her. "We've discovered a castaway colony on the planet. They've done our tests for us by just living here. If there's anything here to catch, they've caught it."

"People on Minos?" Bess's handsome ruddy face grew alive with excitement.

"One of them is down in the medical department," June said. "He'll be out in twenty minutes."

"May I go see him?"

"Sure," said Max. "Show him the way to the dining hall when he gets out. Tell him we sent you."

"Right!" She turned and ran down the ramp like a small girl going to a fire. Max grinned at June and she grinned back. After a year and a half of isolation in space, everyone was hungry for the sight of new faces, the sound of unfamiliar voices.

*

They climbed the last two turns to the cafeteria, and entered to a rich subdued blend of soft music and quiet conversations. The cafeteria was a section of the old dining room, left when the rest of the ship had been converted to living and working quarters, and it still had the original finely grained wood of the ceiling and walls, the sound absorbency, the soft music spools and the intimate small light at each table where people leisurely ate and talked.

They stood in line at the hot foods counter, and behind her June could hear a girl's voice talking excitedly through the murmur of conversation.

"—new man, honest! I saw him through the viewplate when they came in. He's down in the medical department. A real frontiersman."

14

The line drew abreast of the counters, and she and Max chose three heaping trays, starting with hydroponic mushroom steak, raised in the growing trays of water and chemicals; sharp salad bowl with rose tomatoes and aromatic peppers; tank-grown fish with special sauce; four different desserts, and assorted beverages.

Presently they had three tottering trays successfully maneuvered to a table. Brant St. Clair came over. "I beg your pardon, Max, but they are saying something about Reno carrying messages to a colony of savages, for the medical department. Will he be back soon, do you know?"

Max smiled up at him, his square face affectionate. Everyone liked the shy Canadian. "He's back already. We just saw him come in."

"Oh, fine." St. Clair beamed. "I had an appointment with him to go out and confirm what looks like a nice vein of iron to the northeast. Have you seen Bess? Oh—there she is." He turned swiftly and hurried away.

A very tall man with fiery red hair came in surrounded by an eagerly talking crowd of ship people. It was Pat Mead. He stood in the doorway, alertly scanning the dining room. Sheer vitality made him seem even larger than he was. Sighting June, he smiled and began to thread toward their table.

"Look!" said someone. "There's the colonist!" Shelia, a pretty, jeweled woman, followed and caught his arm. "Did you *really* swim across a river to come here?"

Overflowing with good-will and curiosity, people approached from all directions. "Did you actually walk three hundred miles? Come, eat with us. Let me help choose your tray."

Everyone wanted him to eat at their table, everyone was a specialist and wanted data about Minos. They all wanted anecdotes about hunting wild animals with a bow and arrow.

"He needs to be rescued," Max said. "He won't have a chance to eat."

CONTAGION

June and Max got up firmly, edged through the crowd, captured Pat and escorted him back to their table. June found herself pleased to be claiming the hero of the hour.

*

Pat sat in the simple, subtly designed chair and leaned back almost voluptuously, testing the way it gave and fitted itself to him. He ran his eyes over the bright tableware and heaped plates. He looked around at the rich grained walls and soft lights at each table. He said nothing, just looking and feeling and experiencing.

"When we build our town and leave the ship," June explained, "we will turn all the staterooms back into the lounges and ballrooms and cocktail bars that used to be inside."

"Oh, I'm not complaining," Pat said negligently. He cocked his head to the music, and tried to locate its source.

"That's big of you," said Max with gentle irony.

They fell to, Pat beginning the first meal he had had in more than a day.

Most of the other diners finished when they were halfway through, and began walking over, diffidently at first, then in another wave of smiling faces, handshakes, and introductions. Pat was asked about crops, about farming methods, about rainfall and floods, about farm animals and plant breeding, about the compatibility of imported Earth seeds with local ground, about mines and strata.

There was no need to protect him. He leaned back in his chair and drawled answers with the lazy ease of a panther; where he could think of no statistic, he would fill the gap with an anecdote. It developed that he enjoyed spinning campfire yarns and especially being the center of interest.

Between bouts of questions, he ate with undiminished and glowing relish.

June noticed that the female specialists were prolonging the questions more than they needed, clustering around the table laughing at his jokes, until presently Pat was almost surrounded by pretty faces, eager questions, and chiming laughs. Shelia the beautiful laughed most chimingly of all.

June nudged Max, and Max shrugged indifferently. It wasn't anything a man would pay attention to, perhaps. But June watched Pat for a moment more, then glanced uneasily back to Max. He was eating and listening to Pat's answers and did not feel her gaze. For some reason Max looked almost shrunken to her. He was shorter than she had realized; she had forgotten that he was only the same height as herself. She was dimly aware of the clear lilting chatter of female voices increasing at Pat's end of the table.

"That guy's a menace," Max said, and laughed to himself, cutting another slice of hydroponic mushroom steak. "What's eating you?" he added, glancing aside at her when he noticed her sudden stillness.

"Nothing," she said hastily, but she did not turn back to watching Pat Mead. She felt disloyal. Pat was only a superb animal. Max was the man she loved. Or—was he? Of course he was, she told herself angrily. They had gone colonizing together because they wanted to spend their lives together; she had never thought of marrying any other man. Yet the sense of dissatisfaction persisted, and along with it a feeling of guilt.

Len Marlow, the protein tank-culture technician responsible for the mushroom steaks, had wormed his way into the group and asked Pat a question. Now he was saying, "I don't dig you, Pat. It sounds like you're putting the people into the tanks instead of the vegetables!" He glanced at them, looking puzzled. "See if you two can make anything of this. It sounds medical to me."

Pat leaned back and smiled, sipping a glass of hydroponic burgundy. "Wonderful stuff. You'll have to show us how to make it."

Len turned back to him. "You people live off the country, right? You hunt and bring in steaks and eat them, right? Well, say I have one of those steaks right here and I want to eat it, what happens?"

*

"Go ahead and eat it. It just wouldn't digest. You'd stay hungry."

"Why?" Len was aggrieved.

"Chemical differences in the basic protoplasm of Minos. Different amino linkages, left-handed instead of right-handed molecules in the carbohydrates, things like that. Nothing will be digestible here until you are adapted chemically by a little test-tube evolution. Till then you'd starve to death on a full stomach."

Pat's side of the table had been loaded with the dishes from two trays, but it was almost clear now and the dishes were stacked neatly to one side. He started on three desserts, thoughtfully tasting each in turn.

"Test-tube evolution?" Max repeated. "What's that? I thought you people had no doctors."

"It's a story." Pat leaned back again. "Alexander P. Mead, the head of the Mead clan, was a plant geneticist, a very determined personality and no man to argue with. He didn't want us to go through the struggle of killing off all Minos plants and putting in our own, spoiling the face of the planet and upsetting the balance of its ecology. He decided that he would adapt our genes to this planet or kill us trying. He did it all right.'"

"Did which?" asked June, suddenly feeling a sourceless prickle of fear.

"Adapted us to Minos. He took human cells—"

*

She listened intently, trying to find a reason for fear in the explanation. It would have taken many human generations to adapt to Minos by ordinary evolution, and that only at a heavy toll of death and hunger which evolution exacts. There was a shorter way: Human cells have the ability to return to their primeval condition of independence, hunting, eating and reproducing alone.

Alexander P. Mead took human cells and made them into phagocytes. He put them through the hard savage school of evolution—a thousand generations of multiplication, hardship and hunger, with the alien indigestible food always present, offering its reward of plenty to the cell that reluctantly learned to absorb it.

"Leucocytes can run through several thousand generations of evolution in six months," Pat Mead finished. "When they reached to a point where they would absorb Minos food, he planted them back in the people he had taken them from."

"What was supposed to happen then?" Max asked, leaning forward.

"I don't know exactly how it worked. He never told anybody much about it, and when I was a little boy he had gone loco and was wandering ha-ha-ing around waving a test tube. Fell down a ravine and broke his neck at the age of eighty."

"A character," Max said.

Why was she afraid? "It worked then?"

"Yes. He tried it on all the Meads the first year. The other settlers didn't want to be experimented on until they saw how it worked out. It worked. The Meads could hunt, and plant while the other settlers were still eating out of hydroponics tanks."

"It worked," said Max to Len. "You're a plant geneticist and a tank culture expert. There's a job for you."

"Uh-*uh*!" Len backed away. "It sounds like a medical problem to me. Human cell control—right up your alley."

"It is a one-way street," Pat warned. "Once it is done, you won't be able to digest ship food. I'll get no good from this protein. I ate it just for the taste."

Hal Barton appeared quietly beside the table. "Three of the twelve test hamsters have died," he reported, and turned to Pat. "Your people carry the germs of melting sickness, as you call it. The dead hamsters were injected with blood taken from you before you were de-infected. We can't settle here unless we de-infect everybody on Minos. Would they object?"

"We wouldn't want to give you folks germs," Pat smiled. "Anything for safety. But there'll have to be a vote on it first."

CONTAGION

The doctors went to Reno Ulrich's table and walked with him to the hangar, explaining. He was to carry the proposal to Alexandria, mingle with the people, be persuasive and wait for them to vote before returning. He was to give himself shots of cureall every two hours on the hour or run the risk of disease.

*

Reno was pleased. He had dabbled in sociology before retraining as a mechanic for the expedition. "This gives me a chance to study their mores." He winked wickedly. "I may not be back for several nights." They watched through the viewplate as he took off, and then went over to the laboratory for a look at the hamsters.

Three were alive and healthy, munching lettuce. One was the control; the other two had been given shots of Pat's blood from before he entered the ship, but with no additional treatment. Apparently a hamster could fight off melting sickness easily if left alone. Three were still feverish and ruffled, with a low red blood count, but recovering. The three dead ones had been given strong shots of adaptive and counter histamine, so their bodies had not fought back against the attack.

June glanced at the dead animals hastily and looked away again. They lay twisted with a strange semi-fluid limpness, as if ready to dissolve. The last hamster, which had been given the heaviest dose of adaptive, had apparently lost all its hair before death. It was hairless and pink, like a still-born baby.

"We can find no micro-organisms," George Barton said. "None at all. Nothing in the body that should not be there. Leucosis and anemia. Fever only for the ones that fought it off." He handed Max some temperature charts and graphs of blood counts.

June wandered out into the hall. Pediatrics and obstetrics were her field; she left the cellular research to Max, and just helped him with laboratory routine. The strange mood followed her out into the hall, then abruptly lightened.

Coming toward her, busily telling a tale of adventure to the gorgeous Shelia Davenport, was a tall, red-headed, magnificently handsome man. It was his handsomeness which made Pat such a pleasure to look upon and talk with, she guiltily told herself, and it was his tremendous vitality.... It was like meeting a movie hero in the flesh, or a hero out of the pages of a book—Deer-slayer, John Clayton, Lord Greystoke.

She waited in the doorway to the laboratory and made no move to join them, merely acknowledged the two with a nod and a smile and a casual lift of the hand. They nodded and smiled back.

"Hello, June," said Pat and continued telling his tale, but as they passed he lightly touched her arm.

"Oh, pioneer!" she said mockingly and softly to his passing profile, and knew that he had heard.

*

That night she had a nightmare. She was running down a long corridor looking for Max, but every man she came to was a big bronze man with red hair and bright blue eyes who grinned at her.

The pink hamster! She woke suddenly, feeling as if alarm bells had been ringing, and listened carefully, but there was no sound. She had had a nightmare, she told herself, but alarm bells were still ringing in her unconscious. Something was wrong.

Lying still and trying to preserve the images, she groped for a meaning, but the mood faded under the cold touch of reason. Damn intuitive thinking! A pink hamster! Why did the unconscious have to be so vague? She fell asleep again and forgot.

They had lunch with Pat Mead that day, and after it was over Pat delayed June with a hand on her shoulder and looked down at her for a moment. "I want you, June," he said and then turned away, answering the hails of a party at another table as if he had not spoken. She stood shaken, and then walked to the door where Max waited.

21

She was particularly affectionate with Max the rest of the day, and it pleased him. He would not have been if he had known why. She tried to forget Pat's blunt statement.

June was in the laboratory with Max, watching the growth of a small tank culture of the alien protoplasm from a Minos weed, and listening to Len Marlow pour out his troubles.

"And Elsie tags around after that big goof all day, listening to his stories. And then she tells me I'm just jealous, I'm imagining things!" He passed his hand across his eyes. "I came away from Earth to be with Elsie.... I'm getting a headache. Look, can't you persuade Pat to cut it out, June? You and Max are his friends."

"Here, have an aspirin," June said. "We'll see what we can do."

"Thanks." Len picked up his tank culture and went out, not at all cheered.

*

Max sat brooding over the dials and meters at his end of the laboratory, apparently sunk in thought. When Len had gone, he spoke almost harshly.

"Why encourage the guy? Why let him hope?"

"Found out anything about the differences in protoplasm?" she evaded.

"Why let him kid himself? What chance has he got against that hunk of muscle and smooth talk?"

"But Pat isn't after Elsie," she protested.

"Every scatter-brained woman on this ship is trailing after Pat with her tongue hanging out. Brant St. Clair is in the bar right now. He doesn't say what he is drinking about, but do you think Pat is resisting all these women crowding down on him?"

"There are other things besides looks and charm," she said, grimly trying to concentrate on a slide under her binocular microscope.

"Yeah, and whatever they are, Pat has them, too. Who's more competent to support a woman and a family on a frontier planet than a handsome bruiser who was born here?"

"I meant," June spun around on her stool with unexpected passion, "there is old friendship, and there's fondness, and memories, and loyalty!" She was half shouting.

"They're not worth much on the second-hand market," Max said. He was sitting slumped on his lab stool, looking dully at his dials. "Now *I'm* getting a headache!" He smiled ruefully. "No kidding, a real headache. And over other people's troubles yet!"

Other people's troubles.... She got up and wandered out into the long curving halls. "I want you June," Pat's voice repeated in her mind. Why did the man have to be so overpoweringly attractive, so glaring a contrast to Max? Why couldn't the universe manage to run on without generating troublesome love triangles?

*

She walked up the curving ramps to the dining hall where they had eaten and drunk and talked yesterday. It was empty except for one couple talking forehead to forehead over cold coffee.

She turned and wandered down the long easy spiral of corridor to the pharmacy and dispensary. It was empty. George was probably in the test lab next door, where he could hear if he was wanted. The automatic vendor of harmless euphorics, stimulants and opiates stood in the corner, brightly decorated in pastel abstract designs, with its automatic tabulator graph glowing above it.

Max had a headache, she remembered. She recorded her thumbprint in the machine and pushed the plunger for a box of aspirins, trying to focus her attention on the problem of adapting the people of the ship to the planet Minos. An aquarium tank with a faint solution of histamine would be enough to convert a piece of human skin into a community of voracious active phagocytes individually seeking something to devour, but could they eat enough to live away from the rich sustaining plasma of human blood?

After the aspirins, she pushed another plunger for something for herself. Then she stood looking at it, a small box with three pills in her hand—Theobromine, a heart strengthener and a confidence-giving euphoric all in one, something to steady shaky nerves. She had used it before only in emergency. She extended a hand and looked at it. It was trembling. Damn triangles!

While she was looking at her hand there was a click from the automatic drug vendor. It summed the morning use of each drug in the vendors throughout the ship, and recorded it in a neat addition to the end of each graph line. For a moment she could not find the green line for anodynes and the red line for stimulants, and then she saw that they went almost straight up.

There were too many being used—far too many to be explained by jealousy or psychosomatic peevishness. This was an epidemic, and only one disease was possible!

The disinfecting of Pat had not succeeded. Nucleocat Cureall, killer of all infections, had not cured! Pat had brought melting sickness into the ship with him!

Who had it?

The drugs vendor glowed cheerfully, uncommunicative. She opened a panel in its side and looked in on restless interlacing cogs, and on the inside of the door saw printed some directions.... "To remove or examine records before reaching end of the reel—"

After a few fumbling minutes she had the answer. In the cafeteria at breakfast and lunch, thirty-eight men out of the forty-eight aboard ship had taken more than his norm of stimulant. Twenty-one had taken aspirin as well. The only woman who had made an unusual purchase was herself!

She remembered the hamsters that had thrown off the infection with a short sharp fever, and checked back in the records to the day before. There was a short rise in aspirin sales to women at late afternoon. The women were safe.

It was the men who had melting sickness!

Melting sickness killed in hours, according to Pat Mead. How long had the men been sick?

*

As she was leaving, Jerry came into the pharmacy, recorded his thumbprint and took a box of aspirin from the machine.

She felt all right. Self-control was working well and it was pleasant still to walk down the corridor smiling at the people who passed. She took the emergency elevator to the control room and showed her credentials to the technician on watch.

"Medical Emergency." At a small control panel in the corner was a large red button, precisely labeled. She considered it and picked up the control room phone. This was the hard part, telling someone, especially someone who had it—Max.

She dialed, and when the click on the end of the line showed he had picked the phone up, she told Max what she had seen.

"No women, just the men," he repeated. "That right?"

"Yes."

"Probably it's chemically alien, inhibited by one of the female sex hormones. We'll try sex hormone shots, if we have to. Where are you calling from?"

She told him.

"That's right. Give Nucleocat Cureall another chance. It might work this time. Push that button."

She went to the panel and pushed the large red button. Through the long height of the *Explorer*, bells woke to life and began to ring in frightened clangor, emergency doors thumped shut, mechanical apparatus hummed into life and canned voices began to give rapid urgent directions.

A plague had come.

*

She obeyed the mechanical orders, went out into the hall and walked in line with the others. The captain walked ahead of her and the gorgeous Shelia Davenport fell into step beside her. "I look like a positive hag this morning. Does that mean I'm sick? Are we all sick?"

June shrugged, unwilling to say what she knew.

Others came out of all rooms into the corridor, thickening the line. They could hear each room lock as the last person left it, and then, faintly, the hiss of disinfectant spray. Behind them, on the heels of the last person in line, segments of the ship slammed off and began to hiss.

They wound down the spiral corridor until they reached the medical treatment section again, and there they waited in line.

"It won't scar my arms, will it?" asked Shelia apprehensively, glancing at her smooth, lovely arms.

The mechanical voice said, "Next. Step inside, please, and stand clear of the door."

"Not a bit," June reassured Shelia, and stepped into the cubicle.

Inside, she was directed from cubicle to cubicle and given the usual buffeting by sprays and radiation, had blood samples taken and was injected with Nucleocat and a series of other protectives. At last she was directed through another door into a tiny cubicle with a chair.

"You are to wait here," commanded the recorded voice metallically. "In twenty minutes the door will unlock and you may then leave. All people now treated may visit all parts of the ship which have been protected. It is forbidden to visit any quarantine or unsterile part of the ship without permission from the medical officers."

Presently the door unlocked and she emerged into bright lights again, feeling slightly battered.

She was in the clinic. A few men sat on the edge of beds and looked sick. One was lying down. Brant and Bess St. Clair sat near each other, not speaking.

Approaching her was George Barton, reading a thermometer with a puzzled expression.

"What is it, George?" she asked anxiously.

"Some of the women have slight fever, but it's going down. None of the fellows have any—but their white count is way up, their red count is way down, and they look sick to me."

26

She approached St. Clair. His usually ruddy cheeks were pale, his pulse was light and too fast, and his skin felt clammy. "How's the headache? Did the Nucleocat treatment help?"

"I feel worse, if anything."

"Better set up beds," she told George. "Get everyone back into the clinic."

"We're doing that," George assured her. "That's what Hal is doing."

She went back to the laboratory. Max was pacing up and down, absently running his hands through his black hair until it stood straight up. He stopped when he saw her face, and scowled thoughtfully. "They are still sick?" It was more a statement than a question.

She nodded.

"The Cureall didn't cure this time," he muttered. "That leaves it up to us. We have melting sickness and according to Pat and the hamsters, that leaves us less than a day to find out what it is and learn how to stop it."

Suddenly an idea for another test struck him and he moved to the work table to set it up. He worked rapidly, with an occasional uncoordinated movement betraying his usual efficiency.

It was strange to see Max troubled and afraid.

She put on a laboratory smock and began to work. She worked in silence. The mechanicals had failed. Hal and George Barton were busy staving off death from the weaker cases and trying to gain time for Max and her to work. The problem of the plague had to be solved by the two of them alone. It was in their hands.

Another test, no results. Another test, no results. Max's hands were shaking and he stopped a moment to take stimulants.

She went into the ward for a moment, found Bess and warned her quietly to tell the other women to be ready to take over if the men became too sick to go on. "But tell them calmly. We don't want to frighten the men." She lingered in the ward long enough to see the word spread among the women in a widening wave of paler faces and compressed lips; then she went back to the laboratory.

Another test. There was no sign of a micro-organism in anyone's blood, merely a growing horde of leucocytes and phagocytes, prowling as if mobilized to repel invasion.

*

Len Marlow was wheeled in unconscious, with Hal Barton's written comments and conclusions pinned to the blanket.

"I don't feel so well myself," the assistant complained. "The air feels thick. I can't breathe."

June saw that his lips were blue. "Oxygen short," she told Max.

"Low red corpuscle count," Max answered. "Look into a drop and see what's going on. Use mine; I feel the same way he does." She took two drops of Max's blood. The count was low, falling too fast.

Breathing is useless without the proper minimum of red corpuscles in the blood. People below that minimum die of asphyxiation although their lungs are full of pure air. The red corpuscle count was falling too fast. The time she and Max had to work in was too short.

"Pump some more CO_2 into the air system," Max said urgently over the phone. "Get some into the men's end of the ward."

*

She looked through the microscope at the live sample of blood. It was a dark clear field and bright moving things spun and swirled through it, but she could see nothing that did not belong there.

"Hal," Max called over the general speaker system, "cut the other treatments, check for accelerating anemia. Treat it like monoxide poisoning—CO_2 and oxygen."

She reached into a cupboard under the work table, located two cylinders of oxygen, cracked the valves and handed one to Max and one to the assistant. Some of the bluish tint left the assistant's face as he breathed and he went over to the patient with reawakened concern.

"Not breathing, Doc!"

Max was working at the desk, muttering equations of hemoglobin catalysis.

"Len's gone, Doc," the assistant said more loudly.

"Artificial respiration and get him into a regeneration tank," said June, not moving from the microscope. "Hurry! Hal will show you how. The oxidation and mechanical heart action in the tank will keep him going. Put anyone in a tank who seems to be dying. Get some women to help you. Give them Hal's instructions."

The tanks were ordinarily used to suspend animation in a nutrient bath during the regrowth of any diseased organ. It could preserve life in an almost totally destroyed body during the usual disintegration and regrowth treatments for cancer and old age, and it could encourage healing as destruction continued ... but they could not prevent ultimate death as long as the disease was not conquered.

The drop of blood in June's microscope was a great, dark field, and in the foreground, brought to gargantuan solidity by the stereo effect, drifted neat saucer shapes of red blood cells. They turned end for end, floating by the humped misty mass of a leucocyte which was crawling on the cover glass. There were not enough red corpuscles, and she felt that they grew fewer as she watched.

She fixed her eye on one, not blinking in fear that she would miss what might happen. It was a tidy red button, and it spun as it drifted, the current moving it aside in a curve as it passed by the leucocyte.

Then, abruptly, the cell vanished.

June stared numbly at the place where it had been.

Behind her, Max was calling over the speaker system again: "Dr. Stark speaking. Any technician who knows anything about the life tanks, start bringing more out of storage and set them up. Emergency."

"We may need forty-seven," June said quietly.

"We may need forty-seven," Max repeated to the ship in general. His voice did not falter. "Set them up along the corridor. Hook them in on extension lines."

CONTAGION

His voice filtered back from the empty floors above in a series of dim echoes. What he had said meant that every man on board might be on the point of heart stoppage.

*

June looked blindly through the binocular microscope, trying to think. Out of the corner of her eyes she could see that Max was wavering and breathing more and more frequently of the pure, cold, burning oxygen of the cylinders. In the microscope she could see that there were fewer red cells left alive in the drop of his blood. The rate of fall was accelerating.

She didn't have to glance at Max to know how he would look—skin pale, black eyebrows and keen brown eyes slightly squinted in thought, a faint ironical grin twisting the bluing lips. Intelligent, thin, sensitive, his face was part of her mind. It was inconceivable that Max could die. He couldn't die. He couldn't leave her alone.

She forced her mind back to the problem. All the men of the *Explorer* were at the same point, wherever they were.

Moving to Max's desk, she spoke into the intercom system: "Bess, send a couple of women to look through the ship, room by room, with a stretcher. Make sure all the men are down here." She remembered Reno. "Sparks, heard anything from Reno? Is he back?"

Sparks replied weakly after a lag. "The last I heard from Reno was a call this morning. He was raving about mirrors, and Pat Mead's folks not being real people, just carbon copies, and claiming he was crazy; and I should send him the psychiatrist. I thought he was kidding. He didn't call back."

"Thanks, Sparks." Reno was lost.

Max dialed and spoke to the bridge over the phone. "Are you okay up there? Forget about engineering controls. Drop everything and head for the tanks while you can still walk."

June went back to the work table and whispered into her own phone. "Bess, send up a stretcher for Max. He looks pretty bad."

30

There had to be a solution. The life tanks could sustain life in a damaged body, encouraging it to regrow more rapidly, but they merely slowed death as long as the disease was not checked. The postponement could not last long, for destruction could go on steadily in the tanks until the nutritive solution would hold no life except the triumphant microscopic killers that caused melting sickness.

There were very few red blood corpuscles in the microscope field now, incredibly few. She tipped the microscope and they began to drift, spinning slowly. A lone corpuscle floated through the center. She watched it as the current swept it in an arc past the dim off-focus bulk of the leucocyte. There was a sweep of motion and it vanished.

For a moment it meant nothing to her; then she lifted her head from the microscope and looked around. Max sat at his desk, head in hand, his rumpled short black hair sticking out between his fingers at odd angles. A pencil and a pad scrawled with formulas lay on the desk before him. She could see his concentration in the rigid set of his shoulders. He was still thinking; he had not given up.

*

"Max, I just saw a leucocyte grab a red blood corpuscle. It was unbelievably fast."

"Leukemia," muttered Max without moving. "Galloping leukemia yet! That comes under the heading of cancer. Well, that's part of the answer. It might be all we need." He grinned feebly and reached for the speaker set. "Anybody still on his feet in there?" he muttered into it, and the question was amplified to a booming voice throughout the ship. "Hal, are you still going? Look, Hal, change all the dials, change the dials, set them to deep melt and regeneration. One week. This is like leukemia. Got it? This is like leukemia."

June rose. It was time for her to take over the job. She leaned across his desk and spoke into the speaker system. "Doctor Walton talking," she said. "This is to the women. Don't let any of the men work any more; they'll kill themselves. See that they all go into the tanks right away. Set the tank dials for deep regeneration. You can see how from the ones that are set."

Two exhausted and frightened women clattered in the doorway with a stretcher. Their hands were scratched and oily from helping to set up tanks.

"That order includes you," she told Max sternly and caught him as he swayed.

Max saw the stretcher bearers and struggled upright. "Ten more minutes," he said clearly. "Might think of an idea. Something not right in this setup. I have to figure how to prevent a relapse, how the thing started."

He knew more bacteriology than she did; she had to help him think. She motioned the bearers to wait, fixed a breathing mask for Max from a cylinder of CO_2 and the opened one of oxygen. Max went back to his desk.

She walked up and down, trying to think, remembering the hamsters. The melting sickness, it was called. Melting. She struggled with an impulse to open a tank which held one of the men. She wanted to look in, see if that would explain the name.

Melting Sickness....

Footsteps came and Pat Mead stood uncertainly in the doorway. Tall, handsome, rugged, a pioneer. "Anything I can do?" he asked.

She barely looked at him. "You can stay out of our way. We're busy."

"I'd like to help," he said.

"Very funny." She was vicious, enjoying the whip of her words. "Every man is dying because you're a carrier, and you want to help."

*

He stood nervously clenching and unclenching his hands. "A guinea pig, maybe. I'm immune. All the Meads are."

"Go away." God, why couldn't she think? What makes a Mead immune?

32

"Aw, let 'im alone," Max muttered. "Pat hasn't done anything." He went waveringly to the microscope, took a tiny sliver from his finger, suspended it in a slide and slipped it under the lens with detached habitual dexterity. "Something funny going on," he said to June. "Symptoms don't feel right."

After a moment he straightened and motioned for her to look. "Leucocytes, phagocytes—" He was bewildered. "My own—"

She looked in, and then looked back at Pat in a growing wave of horror. "They're not your own, Max!" she whispered.

Max rested a hand on the table to brace himself, put his eye to the microscope, and looked again. June knew what he saw. Phagocytes, leucocytes, attacking and devouring his tissues in a growing incredible horde, multiplying insanely.

Not his phagocytes! Pat Mead's! The Meads' evolved cells had learned too much. They were contagious. And not Pat Mead's.... How much alike *were* the Meads?... Mead cells contagious from one to another, not a disease attacking or being fought, but acting as normal leucocytes in whatever body they were in! The leucocytes of tall, red-headed people, finding no strangeness in the bloodstream of any of the tall, red-headed people. No strangeness.... A toti-potent leucocyte finding its way into cellular wombs.

The womblike life tanks. For the men of the *Explorer*, a week's cure with deep melting to de-differentiate the leucocytes and turn them back to normal tissue, then regrowth and reforming from the cells that were there. From the cells that *were* there. *From the cells that were there....*

"Pat—"

"I know." Pat began to laugh, his face twisted with sudden understanding. "I understand. I get it. I'm a contagious personality. That's funny, isn't it?"

Max rose suddenly from the microscope and lurched toward him, fists clenched. Pat caught him as he fell, and the bewildered stretcher bearers carried him out to the tanks.

CONTAGION

For a week June tended the tanks. The other women volunteered to help, but she refused. She said nothing, hoping her guess would not be true.

"Is everything all right?" Elsie asked her anxiously. "How is Jerry coming along?" Elsie looked haggard and worn, like all the women, from doing the work that the men had always done.

"He's fine," June said tonelessly, shutting tight the door of the tank room. "They're all fine."

"That's good," Elsie said, but she looked more frightened than before.

June firmly locked the tank room door and the girl went away.

The other women had been listening, and now they wandered back to their jobs, unsatisfied by June's answer, but not daring to ask for the actual truth. They were there whenever June went into the tank room, and they were still there—or relieved by others; June was not sure—when she came out. And always some one of them asked the unvarying question for all the others, and June gave the unvarying answer. But she kept the key. No woman but herself knew what was going on in the life tanks.

Then the day of completion came. June told no one of the hour. She went into the room as on the other days, locked the door behind her, and there was the nightmare again. This time it was reality and she wandered down a path between long rows of coffinlike tanks, calling, "Max! Max!" silently and looking into each one as it opened.

But each face she looked at was the same. Watching them dissolve and regrow in the nutrient solution, she had only been able to guess at the horror of what was happening. Now she knew.

They were all the same lean-boned, blond-skinned face, with a pin-feather growth of reddish down on cheeks and scalp. All horribly—and handsomely—the same.

A medical kit lay carelessly on the floor beside Max's tank. She stood near the bag. "Max," she said, and found her throat closing.

34

The canned voice of the mechanical mocked her, speaking glibly about waking and sitting up. "I'm sorry, Max...."

The tall man with rugged features and bright blue eyes sat up sleepily and lifted an eyebrow at her, and ran his hand over his red-fuzzed head in a gesture of bewilderment.

"What's the matter, June?" he asked drowsily.

She gripped his arm. "Max—"

He compared the relative size of his arm with her hand and said wonderingly, "You shrank."

"I know, Max. I know."

He turned his head and looked at his arms and legs, pale blond arms and legs with a down of red hair. He touched the thick left arm, squeezed a pinch of hard flesh. "It isn't mine," he said, surprised. "But I can feel it."

Watching his face was like watching a stranger mimicking and distorting Max's expressions. Max in fear. Max trying to understand what had happened to him, looking around at the other men sitting up in their tanks. Max feeling the terror that was in herself and all the men as they stared at themselves and their friends and saw what they had become.

"We're all Pat Mead," he said harshly. "All the Meads are Pat Mead. That's why he was surprised to see people who didn't look like himself."

"Yes, Max."

"Max," he repeated. "It's me, all right. The nervous system didn't change." His new blue eyes held hers. "My love didn't, either. Did yours? Did it, June?"

"No, Max." But she couldn't know yet. She had loved Max with the thin, ironic face, the rumpled black hair and the twisted smile that never really hid his quick sympathy. Now he was Pat Mead. Could he also be Max? "Of course I still love you, darling."

He grinned. It was still the wry smile of Max, though fitting strangely on the handsome new blond face. "Then it isn't so bad. It might even be pretty good. I envied him this big, muscular body. If Pat or any of these Meads so much as looks at you, I'm going to knock his block off. Understand?"

*

She laughed and couldn't stop. It wasn't that funny. But it was still Max, trying to be unafraid, drawing on humor. Maybe the rest of the men would also be their old selves, enough so the women would not feel that their men were strangers.

Behind her, male voices spoke characteristically. She did not have to turn to know which was which: "This is one way to keep a guy from stealing your girl," that was Len Marlow; "I've got to write down all my reactions," Hal Barton; "Now I can really work that hillside vein of metal," St. Clair. Then others complaining, swearing, laughing bitterly at the trick that had been played on them and their flirting, tempted women. She knew who they were. Their women would know them apart, too.

"We'll go outside," Max said. "You and I. Maybe the shock won't be so bad to the women after they see me." He paused. "You didn't tell them, did you?"

"I couldn't. I wasn't sure. I—was hoping I was wrong."

She opened the door and closed it quickly. There was a small crowd on the other side.

"Hello, Pat," Elsie said uncertainly, trying to look past them into the tank room before the door shut.

"I'm not Pat, I'm Max," said the tall man with the blue eyes and the fuzz-reddened skull. "Listen—"

"Good heavens, Pat, what happened to your hair?" Shelia asked.

"I'm Max," insisted the man with the handsome face and the sharp blue eyes. "Don't you get it? I'm Max Stark. The melting sickness is Mead cells. We caught them from Pat. They adapted us to Minos. They also changed us all into Pat Mead."

The women stared at him, at each other. They shook their heads.

"They don't understand," June said. "I couldn't have if I hadn't seen it happening, Max."

"It's Pat," said Shelia, dazedly stubborn. "He shaved off his hair. It's some kind of joke."

Max shook her shoulders, glaring down at her face. "I'm Max. Max Stark. They all look like me. Do you hear? It's funny, but it's not a joke. Laugh for us, for God's sake!"

"It's too much," said June. "They'll have to see."

She opened the door and let them in. They hurried past her to the tanks, looking at forty-six identical blond faces, beginning to call in frightened voices:

"Jerry!"

"Harry!"

"Lee, where are you, sweetheart—"

June shut the door on the voices that were growing hysterical, the women terrified and helpless, the men shouting to let the women know who they were.

"It isn't easy," said Max, looking down at his own thick muscles. "But you aren't changed and the other girls aren't. That helps."

Through the muffled noise and hysteria, a bell was ringing.

"It's the airlock," June said.

Peering in the viewplate were nine Meads from Alexandria. To all appearances, eight of them were Pat Mead at various ages, from fifteen to fifty, and the other was a handsome, leggy, red-headed girl who could have been his sister.

Regretfully, they explained through the voice tube that they had walked over from Alexandria to bring news that the plane pilot had contracted melting sickness there and had died.

They wanted to come in.

*

June and Max told them to wait and returned to the tank room. The men were enjoying their new height and strength, and the women were bewilderedly learning that they could tell one Pat Mead from another, by voice, by gesture of face or hand. The panic was gone. In its place was a dull acceptance of the fantastic situation.

Max called for attention. "There are nine Meads outside who want to come in. They have different names, but they're all Pat Mead."

They frowned or looked blank, and George Barton asked, "Why didn't you let them in? I don't see any problem."

"One of them," said Max soberly, "is a girl. *Patricia* Mead. The girl wants to come in."

There was a long silence while the implication settled to the fear center of the women's minds. Shelia the beautiful felt it first. She cried, "No! Please don't let her in!" There was real fright in her tone and the women caught it quickly.

Elsie clung to Jerry, begging, "You don't want me to change, do you, Jerry? You like me the way I am! Tell me you do!"

*

The other girls backed away. It was illogical, but it was human. June felt terror rising in herself. She held up her hand for quiet, and presented the necessity to the group.

"Only half of us can leave Minos," she said. "The men cannot eat ship food; they've been conditioned to this planet. We women can go, but we would have to go without our men. We can't go outside without contagion, and we can't spend the rest of our lives in quarantine inside the ship. George Barton is right—there is no problem."

"But we'd be changed!" Shelia shrilled. "I don't want to become a Mead! I don't want to be somebody else!"

She ran to the inner wall of the corridor. There was a brief hesitation, and then, one by one, the women fled to that side, until there were only Bess, June and four others left.

"See!" cried Shelia. "A vote! We can't let the girl in!"

No one spoke. To change, to be someone else—the idea was strange and horrifying. The men stood uneasily glancing at each other, as if looking into mirrors, and against the wall of the corridor the women watched in fear and huddled together, staring at the men. One man in forty-seven poses. One of them made a beseeching move toward Elsie and she shrank away.

"No, Jerry! I won't let you change me!"

Max stirred restlessly, the ironic smile that made his new face his own unconsciously twisting into a grimace of pity. "We men can't leave, and you women can't stay," he said bluntly. "Why not let Patricia Mead in. Get it over with!"

June took a small mirror from her belt pouch and studied her own face, aware of Max talking forcefully, the men standing silent, the women pleading. Her face ... her own face with its dark blue eyes, small nose, long mobile lips ... the mind and the body are inseparable; the shape of a face is part of the mind. She put the mirror back.

"I'd kill myself!" Shelia was sobbing. "I'd rather die!"

"You won't die," Max was saying. "Can't you see there's only one solution—"

They were looking at Max. June stepped silently out of the tank room, and then turned and went to the airlock. She opened the valves that would let in Pat Mead's sister.

CONTAGION

www.ingramcontent.com/pod-product-compliance
Lightning Source LLC
Chambersburg PA
CBHW050917120626
46552CB00004B/1624